GHOSTED

GHOSTED

MICHAEL FRY

HOUGHTON MIFFLIN HARCOURT
BOSTON   NEW YORK

Text and illustrations copyright © 2021 by Houghton Mifflin Harcourt

All rights reserved. For information about permission to reproduce
selections from this book, write to trade.permissions@hmhco.com or
to Permissions, Houghton Mifflin Harcourt Publishing Company,
3 Park Avenue, 19th Floor, New York, New York 10016.

hmhbooks.com

The text was set in Adobe Garamond Pro.
Design by Natalie Fondriest

Library of Congress Cataloging-in-Publication Data is available.
ISBN 978-0-358-26961-8

Manufactured in the United States of America
DOC 10 9 8 7 6 5 4 3 2 1
4500814614

For Kim

CHAPTER 1

I first met Grimm in fourth grade.

I was at lunch. Normally my mom gives me money for lunch, but that morning she was out of cash, so she made my lunch.

My mom is a lovely person with many fine qualities. Making nutritious lunches is not one of them. But to be fair, I didn't mind. A jar of peanut butter and a warm soda beats cafeteria mystery soup any day of the week.

I was just about to open the warm soda when it slipped out of my hand.

There was silence. Everyone knew I'd just let loose a live soda grenade in the cafeteria.

I was suddenly alone with a warm soda bomb of my own making. Or so I thought.

"Why didn't you run away with the others?" I asked.

"You looked like you needed some help," he said. "Also, I'm an expert at bomb disposal."

"It's not a bomb. It's a can of warm soda."

"If we don't get it out of here and it explodes, you're going to be in detention for a month."

That's when we heard a metallic . . .

"We don't have much time," said the kid.

"Do I know you?" I asked.

"First thing we need is body armor," said Grimm.

"Body armor?" I said.

"Let's see," said Grimm, looking around the cafeteria. "This should work."

SOUP BOWL

OH.

BACKWARDS BACKPACK

I found a bowl and a backpack and suited up as well.

"Now what?" I asked.

Grimm said, "We need a couple of those long lunch-lady spoons."

Right. The kind they use to stir the Monkey Eye Soup.

We found two spoons and approached the vending machine.

"This is a delicate operation," said Grimm. "We have to move as one. You grab one side of the can; I'll grab the other."

We both reached under the vending machine and pinched the can between the two spoons.

We slowly pulled out the can. Then, very carefully, we stood up.

The can could have exploded at any second. It was about one hundred yards from where we were to the school's back door and the soccer field beyond. We each took a deep breath, then carefully, oh so carefully, picked up the can again and slowly started to move. We looked like two deranged giant mice tiptoeing down the hall.

"Thanks," I said. "You really didn't need to help me with this."

"Are you kidding? This is a blast!" said Grimm.

We got out the back door and headed straight to the soccer field as carefully as we could.

From that point on we were best friends forever. Pinky-swear friends. Spit-shake friends. And walla-walla-elbow-bump friends.

The Warm Soda Grenade Incident was just the first of many adventures.

In fifth grade our big adventure was climbing the water tower. No big deal. Walk in the park. Piece of cake.

WE'RE ALL GOING TO DIE!!

In sixth grade we painted ourselves silver and pretended to be statues in the park.

This fooled only the pigeons.

This year we topped ourselves. We decided to dig a hole to China. This was Grimm's idea. I was a bit skeptical that China was within digging distance.

GURGLE GURGLE

We were both grounded for life after that, but it was worth it. We made the local news.

AREA BOYS DIG TUNNEL TO CHINA AND ALMOST DROWN.

We had a great time together. Grimm helped me get out of my shell. Normally, I kind of blended into the background.

And when he needed it, I provided him with cover.

We had so much fun that we made a list of future adventures. We called it our Totally To-Do List.

A couple of weeks ago we made plans for the spaghetti bath thing. We were all set. We had the spaghetti. We had the tub. Mom was at yoga class. There was just one problem. No Grimm. He didn't show. Which was weird. He always shows.

I called his phone. No answer. I went to his house down the block to get him. It had been a stormy day. A big thunderstorm had blown through. Noisy. Lots of lightning.

As I approached Grimm's house, I could see a fire truck. But I didn't smell smoke. I just smelled that nice after-storm smell. Rain-rinsed air. Sparkly. Like just-washed underwear out of the dryer. It smelled calm.

And safe.

And happy.

And then I blinked. I saw the ambulance. I saw Grimm's mom crying. And I knew in my gut that my best friend was . . .

... GONE?

CHAPTER 2

Yup. Grimm, my best friend in the entire universe, died two weeks ago saving a cat during a thunder-storm.

Who does that?

This guy.

I felt like I'd lost my right elbow, part of my left knee, and a couple of toenails.

I sat in our treehouse and stared at the cat Grimm had rescued.

"I lose Grimm and I get you?" I said out loud.

I guess getting stuck in a tree in a lightning storm is just what stray cats do.

"It's not the cat's fault," said a super-familiar voice.

"What?" I whispered.

"It was Mr. Vogal's peek-a-pit bull's fault. Mr. Sniggles chased it up the tree. I had to save it. The odds of getting hit by lightning are a million to one. Who knew I was so attractive?"

"Grimm?" I whispered.

"You don't need to whisper," said Grimm. "I'm standing right here."

I turned around and there he was.

And then I screamed.

I know. Screaming is not a good look for a twelve-year-old boy, but when your dead friend is standing right in front of you, what are you going to do?

"Larry, stop!" yelled Grimm.

I stopped. Then I stared.

"You're . . . you're . . . dead," I stammered.

"Sort of dead."

"All the way dead."

"Kind of dead."

"Super dead."

"Dead-ish."

Grimm put his hands up. "Dude, chill!"

Well, I *was* shaking, that's sort of chill-ish, but probably not what he meant.

Grimm said, "I'm standing right in front of you. I'm talking. I'm seeing. I'm hearing . . .

"*Mostly* real," he added.

"You're a ghost," I said.

"I know! How cool is that?"

I had to think about that. On the one hand, Grimm was a ghost, which was weird. But then again, Grimm had always been weird, so was this really any weirder? And besides, he was my best friend, and he was back.

Sure, back from the dead, but . . . you know . . . it was still pretty awesome.

"Pretty cool," I agreed.

"You're sort of back."

"Dude, I'm a ghost!"

"What does that mean?"

"I don't know. I've never been a ghost before."

"Isn't there online help? Customer service? Some sort of manual?"

"No. I was alive. Then I died. Now I'm here. You're the first person, dead or alive, that I've talked to."

"You don't remember anything?"

"I remember saving the cat. Then the lightning. Then I was here."

"Dying is weird."

"I know!"

"Okay," I said. "We can figure this out."

"I don't want to haunt anybody."

"Why not?"

"It's creepy and weird. I mean, I wouldn't want anyone to haunt me."

"Right. We'll put haunting aside. Can you float?"

"Can you float through walls?"

"Can you say 'Boo'?"

"Now what?" I said.

Grimm shrugged. "I dunno. I've never been dead before."

"I guess we can hang out," I suggested.

"Yeah. Like your wingman. I can keep an eye out for stuff. You know, stop you before you tap Christi Mathison on the shoulder again and she turns at the last second and you shove your finger up her nose."

"I thought you said you didn't want to haunt anybody."

"Sorry," said Grimm. "I promise, no haunting."

"Honey, it's time to come in for dinner," yelled my mom from below.

"Hide!" I whispered. "She's coming up the ladder!"

Grimm looked around. "Where?"

Too late. Mom poked her head up through the trapdoor.

"Are you okay, honey?" she asked.

I paused for a moment. Then, in my very best everything's-okay voice, I said, "I'm fine. Why wouldn't I be okay?"

"Um . . . well, you know . . . Grimm?" said Mom.

I closed my eyes. "Oh. Right."

Mom continued. "I mean, you're spending all your time in this treehouse with that soggy cat."

"Meow!" objected the cat.

"I'm okay," I said.

"Well, hurry up, your beets are getting cold," she said as she left.

"Mmm . . . beets," whispered Grimm.

"She didn't see you!" I said.

"Yeah. I guess only you can see me."

MEOW!

"And the cat," I said.

"You should probably go eat your beets," said Grimm.

"What are you going to do?"

"I dunno. Be a ghost. Practice my boos. Float menacingly. Figure out if I should wear a sheet. Are sheets even a thing? There's so much I don't know about being dead."

I didn't know what to say. I mean, I was happy Grimm was back. I'd really missed him. And now he was right in front of me. It was like Christmas.

On Mars.

What do you say to your dead best friend who's now a ghost?

I said, "Do you want me to bring you some beets?"

Grimm shook his head. "I'm good."

We stared at each other for a beat (not a beet). Then we both started to smile. Then, despite all the weirdness, we had the same thought.

"Pretty awesome," I said.

Grimm nodded. "Awesomazing!"

"Is that a word?"

"It's a ghost word. A ghost word I made up."

"Whoa."

"I know. Ghosts have skills."

I started to climb down the ladder. "Can you make my beets disappear?"

"No."

"You can't or you won't?"

"Eat your beets, Larry."

WELCOME BACK, GRIMM.

GOOD TO BE BACK!

CHAPTER 3

Okay. That whole best-friend-comes-back-as-a-ghost thing? Yeah, *that* was weird.

Not weird like Great-Aunt-Jenny weird. My Great Aunt Jenny sleeps with cookie dough on her face. She says by morning the cookie dough is gone, and she feels rested and refreshed.

No, I mean weird like DEAD-FRIENDS-ARE
NOT-SUPPOSED-TO-COME-BACK-TO-LIFE
weird!

Later that night, I started to think maybe it was all
a bad dream. Maybe I'd had a bad beet and I halluci-
nated the whole thing. After all, I was an anxious sort.

Nope. Not a dream. Or a hallucination.

"What?" I whispered.

Grimm said, "I'm bored."

"You're a ghost. Scare someone!"

"I just did. It's boring."

"What is wrong with you?"

"Hey, it's okay."

"I just went to my house. I watched my mom and dad sleep. Well, Dad was asleep, but Mom just lay there wide awake. I tried to talk to her, but she couldn't hear me."

"I'm here, but I'm not here. Why?"

"I don't know," I said.

"Where are all the other ghosts? I mean, people and pets die all the time. I should be running into ghost goldfish all over the place."

"I guess they passed on."

"The goldfish passed on, but I didn't."

"Grimm, we'll figure this out," I said, a little too loudly.

"Larry, are you okay?" said my mom from outside my room.

"Hide!" I said to Grimm.

"You know she can't see me," said Grimm.

The doorknob turned.

"HIDE!" I hissed.

Grimm rolled his eyes as he slid under the bed.

Mom entered the room. "Who are you talking to, Larry?"

"Myself," I said.

"I think maybe you should see someone."

"See who?"

"Someone to talk to . . . I mean, other than yourself."

Grimm popped up from under the bed. "I agree."

"Shut up!" I whispered.

"Larry! You don't tell me to shut up," said Mom.

I waved my hands. "No. Mom. I was talking to . . ."

"Who were you talking to?" asked Mom.

YES, LARRY...
WHO WERE YOU
TALKING TO?

"Okay," I said. "Hold on. I'm stressed. My best friend died. It's weird, is all. I'll be fine."

"It's okay," said Mom.

I said, "No, it really isn't okay. It just is."

Mom took a deep breath. "You've lost your best friend. It's only been a couple of weeks. It takes time."

"And then what happens?" I asked.

"It gets better," said Mom. "I promise."

"Pinky swear?"

Mom leaned down.

Mom left my room and closed the door behind her.

Grimm said, "Aw, that was sweet."

"Please go away," I said.

"That's just it. I can't."

I sighed. "I know."

We sat there for a second, not saying anything.

"Again," I said, "we're going to figure this out."

Grimm looked worried. "Promise?"

"Promise," I said. "Now go find something to do until morning."

"What? I can't sleep."

"Wait, I know! We've been having trouble with raccoons getting into the trash at night. Try scaring them off."

"I don't know," said Grimm as he went to the window to look outside. "Can they even see me?"

"The cat can see you."

"Also, they look really mean."

"They can't hurt you," I reminded him.

"Oh. Right."

I watched him pass through the window and go outside. I got up to make sure he was all right.

It was going to be a long night.

CHAPTER 4

"You drool in your sleep," said Grimm.

It was the next morning. A Saturday, so no school. We were back in the treehouse. Me and my best friend, who happened to be a ghost. Just hanging out.

As you do.

"And you twitch your leg like a dog when you're dreaming," he added.

"Did you watch me sleep *all* night?" I asked.

"No, not all night. I was in the bathroom for a little while."

"Why?"

"I was curious to see if ghosts can pee."

I closed my eyes. "I can't believe I'm having this conversation."

Grimm didn't say anything.

"Well?" I said.

"Well what?" asked Grimm.

"DO GHOSTS PEE?"

"No," said Grimm. "And you know what? You really don't miss a thing until it's gone."

"Meow," agreed the cat.

"Can we change the subject?" I asked.

"Sure. What do you want to talk about?"

"How about the elephant in the room?"

"Here? In the room? A ghost elephant? Why can't I see it?"

"No, dummy. You! We should talk about you . . . being a ghost."

"Just so I'm clear, there's no ghost elephant."

"THERE'S NO GHOST ELEPHANT!"

"You don't have to yell."

"Last night, you were wondering why you're still here and all the other ghosts are gone."

"Yeah."

"Maybe you have *unfinished business*."

"I'm just a kid. What sort of business would I leave unfinished?"

"Well, you never did your homework. Or studied for a test. You borrowed two dollars from me that one time and never paid me back. And . . . you ruined my scout knife when you used it to carve your initials into the new sidewalk at school."

Grimm put his hands up. "Not my fault. That cement dried really quickly."

"The point is," I said, "all of that is unfinished business."

"No, not really. I think unfinished business should have something to do with regret, and I don't regret any of those things. It should be something you're desperate to do over, or . . ."

Grimm was staring at the wall next to me.

". . . something that you're desperate to do in the first place."

I turned around.

It was the Totally To-Do List (illustrated by yours truly). Could that be the unfinished business? I mean, we'd done some of it. We ran a Tough Mudder (the dirt still comes out when I floss) and we rode the Deathcoaster (I only threw up once). But we never finished it.

"I don't know," I said. "Is not ever taking a bath in spaghetti really 'unfinished business'?"

Grimm smiled. "I really, really regret not ever taking a bath in spaghetti."

"You're so weird," I said.

"Meow," agreed the cat again.

"But wait," said Grimm. "Now we can do it. We can fill a bath with spaghetti . . . or, you know, linguini."

"You can't take a bath in anything," I pointed out. "You're not real. You can't feel it. Because you're not *really* here."

"I'm here. That's the problem."

"You know what I mean. It's not happening to you."

"But it could happen to *you!*"

That was true. Of all the stuff on the list, taking a bath in spaghetti was the one I was most curious about. Sure, it was gross. But was it a cool kind of gross? Or a gross kind of gross? Only one way to find out.

"Okay," I said. "I'm game, but do we have to do the *whole* list? There's some scary stuff on this list."

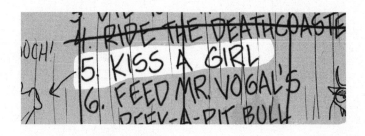

Seriously scary stuff.

"Let's take it one item at a time," said Grimm. "Maybe it'll just take one. Maybe it'll take a bunch. I don't know. I've never done this before."

I shook my head.

Grimm smiled.

"Meow," offered the cat.

"I don't know if we still have enough spaghetti," I said.

"You could kiss a girl first," said Grimm.

I swear the cat smiled.

CHAPTER 5

We had to wait until Mom went to yoga.

We didn't have enough spaghetti. We had to use ra-
men noodles and some gluten-free lasagna and some
mac *without* the cheese dust. Fortunately, we had a
crate of mac and cheese from Costco.

We boiled it all up in a couple of huge lobster pots.

"How do we know if it's ready?" I asked.

Grimm said, "You throw it against the refrigerator and see if it sticks."

"What if I throw it against you and see if it sticks?"

"Then we'd have ghost pasta, and who knows how we'd get rid of that?"

I laughed. Then Grimm laughed. Good times. Good *weird* times.

We strained the pots and proceeded to the bathroom. They were heavy. We needed some help.

"How much time do we have?" asked Grimm.

I said, "Plenty. My mom won't be back for an hour."

We sloshed some boiled-pasta water on the hall carpet on the way to the bathroom. Grimm assured me that boiled-pasta water doesn't stain. I asked him how he could be sure. He said, "The dead tell no tales."

Good enough for me.

Finally, we arrived at the bathroom.

"If this works, you'll move on," I said.

"Yeah," said Grimm. "I guess so."

We stood there and stared at each other for a beat.

I said, "I'd give you a hug, but it feels weird just hugging air."

"I understand," said Grimm.

"I hope you have a safe trip."

"A safe trip?"

"You know, to heaven."

"I wonder what it'll be like." said Grimm.

"Nice. Though probably no one's taking baths in pasta," I offered.

I turned to leave.

"Where are you going?" asked Grimm.

I said. "I'm going to get my bathing suit."

"Why?"

"I'm not taking a bath in spaghetti naked."

"But what if that's the thing?"

"What thing?"

"The thing that makes the difference. What if the

only way I can pass on is if you take a bath naked in spaghetti?"

"That's crazy," I said.

Grimm shrugged. "Hey, I don't make the rules."

"THERE ARE NO RULES!"

"Good point."

"I tell you what," I said. "I'll do it in swim trunks, and then if you don't pass on I'll do it naked."

"Okay."

"But you have to leave the bathroom."

"But what if I have to BE in the bathroom for it to work?"

"Do you want to see me naked?"

"Not really."

"Good. We're agreed."

I left and put on my swim trunks. When I returned, Grimm was hovering over the tub.

"I'm going to miss taking baths," he said.

"In spaghetti?"

"Sure."

"I'll describe it to you."

"That would be nice."

I dumped the spaghetti in the tub. It made a big SPLOOSH as it filled up about half the tub. I stepped inside.

I started giggling. Grimm joined in.
"Be serious," I said.
Grimm smiled. "You first."
I sat down in the tub.

"You know, it's interesting. Like a noodle blanket. The spaghetti sort of goes everywhere . . ."

"That's enough describing," said Grimm.

We waited for a minute or so. Nothing happened.

I said, "You're still here."

Grimm nodded. "Yes, I am. Guess it's time to get naked."

"I really don't like you right now."

"I understand, but we should try everything."

I sighed. This whole situation was out of control. But who knew? Maybe sitting in pasta naked would do the trick.

"Well?" I said.

"Well, what?" said Grimm.

"Get out!"

"Right."

Grimm left the bathroom. I took off my trunks and sat back down in the damp pasta. It tickled. But I didn't laugh.

"You still there?" I yelled.

"Give it a minute," Grimm yelled back.

A minute. Sure. I'll just sit here naked in wet pasta for a minute.

I wondered if I could have my memory of all this erased. Was that a thing? That should really be a thing.

A minute was up.

"Grimm?" I yelled. "You there?"

Nothing.

"Grimm? Stop messing with me!"

Still nothing.

Could this have actually worked? I immediately felt bad. My best friend was gone. He was here. Then he was gone. Then he was back. Then he was gone again. Gone forever this time. I don't cry often, but the tears welled up in my eyes. I guess it was all for the best. But then why did the best feel like the worst?

Man, the universe was weird.

One more time. "Grimm?"

The bathroom door opened. Mom came in.

HONEY, GRIMM ISN'T HERE.

UH-OH...

CHAPTER 6

"What are you doing here?" I cried.

Mom said, "I forgot my yoga blocks. What are *you* doing there?"

I CAN EXPLAIN.

Grimm smiled. "This is going to be fun."

"Is that my gluten-free lasagna?" asked Mom.

"Yes," I said.

"I think it's time you talk to Dr. Hank."

Dr. Hank was a psychologist I saw for a couple of weeks because of this no-big-deal panic attack I had once.

Okay, so I have a thing about spiders and gym. But mostly gym.

Anyway, this was not good. Nothing about this was good. Whatever I came up with in this moment was going to have to be spectacular. Otherwise I was going to be parked at Dr. Hank's, "dialoguing" about "life" for the rest of my life.

I decided to tell the truth.

Sort of.

"You know how Grimm and I have our Totally To-Do List written on the side of the treehouse?" I asked.

"No, but okay," said Mom.

"It's this list," I said. "Of all the things we were going to do together."

"A list?"

"Yeah. Stupid stuff. You know, 'Eat a ghost pepper,' 'Build a Parthenon out of used gum'—"

"Take a bath naked in pasta?"

"Right. First on the list."

"And you thought taking a bath in pasta would bring Grimm back?"

"No! Of course not! That's ridiculous," I said.

Look at me! Telling the truth! Sort of.

"But I heard you calling out for Grimm," said Mom.

I didn't say anything. Maybe it was time to tell the whole truth.

"I miss him," I said.

Mom smiled. "I know, honey."

"I just thought . . . I know it's dumb . . . but I thought if I did some stuff on the list, it might make me feel closer to Grimm."

I paused.

"And it did."

"I understand," said Mom.

Whoa. You do?

Mom continued. "But it looks to me like you're having a rough time with all of this, and you should talk to someone. Someone like Dr. Hank."

"I'll think about it," I said.

"Good," said Mom. "Now, clean this mess up, then take a proper bath, and then maybe a nap . . . or some quiet time . . . or, you know, something."

"Sure," I said. "Are you going on to yoga?"

"No. I don't think this is a good time to leave you alone."

Groan.

"Honey, it's all going to be okay."

"Sure," I said.

Mom left. I was alone. Well, not entirely alone.

CHAPTER 7

"I'm not bathing in any more pasta," I said.

Grimm agreed. "Fine. We can cross that one off."

It was later that afternoon. We were back in the treehouse.

I said, "Maybe we should forget about the list."

"Why?" asked Grimm. "The list could be the key to my moving on."

"That's just it. Do you *have* to move on?"

"You don't want me to move on?"

"Sure . . . I mean, if you want. Or, if you have to. Do you have to?"

"I don't know. This whole dead thing is new to me."

This was a weird moment. I wanted him to stay. I mean, if he wanted to stay. But I also wanted what was best for him. And maybe moving on was for the best.

I said, "It's just . . . you know, it's okay if you want to stay, but . . ."

"But what?"

"But maybe you're supposed to move on."

I looked at the list on the treehouse wall again.

Grimm couldn't *do* any of those things. All he could do was watch. And . . . give advice. About kissing, for instance.

PILLOW

I THINK IT'S LIKE BLOWING UP A BALLOON EXCEPT OPPOSITE.

"Never mind," I said. "You should move on."

"Only if you want me to," said Grimm.

"Yes. I definitely want you to move on. For sure. Absolutely."

"Now what?"

"I guess we keep going on the list."

Grimm pointed at my face. "By the way, you have something on your lip."

I wiped my face with the back of my hand.

"Thanks."

"You're welcome."

Grimm just stared at me for a few seconds.

"What are you doing?"

"Well, a random act of kindness didn't do the trick. I'm still here. Six down. Thirty-two to go."

I looked at the list again. There was a lot of silly stuff on it.

But there was also a lot of serious stuff.

8. BECOME BLOOD BROTHERS.
14. MAKE AN UGLY PLACE
    BEAUTIFUL.
23. BUILD SOME
    MUSCLES.

GRR..

And a lot of this stuff had to do with school.

13. TRY OUT FOR A TEAM.
16. PRANK MS. SPITZCRACKER.
24. TALK TO EVERY KID
    IN SCHOOL.

↳ HEY. HEY.

"Okay," I said. "We keep trying."

Grimm smiled. "That's the spirit! I mean, I'm the spirit. I mean . . . you know what I mean."

The cat nodded. The cat knew what he meant.

"Okay," I said. "But we're going to do this my way. No more getting walked in on by Mom. Any of the really stupid or silly stuff, we do it up here in the treehouse. At night. With the lights off. And no cellphones."

Grimm looked confused. "Why?"

NO PICTURES!

"Got it," said Grimm.

"Also, we go slow. We work out a timeline. I'll make a spreadsheet to record results. And, of course, safety first. I'll need a headlamp. Some rope. A whistle. Maybe one of those orange-and-yellow vests."

"Larry?"

"Yes, Grimm?"

"It's okay."

"What do you mean?"

"I can sense that you're nervous. It's going to be okay," said Grimm. "We'll figure this out together. You'll be fine."

"We'll be fine."

"I'm dead, Larry."

"But I might have to KISS A GIRL!"

"It's not a competition, Larry."

We spent the rest of the day thinking and planning. We went over the list and decided on what we'd try next. Grimm made it through the night without too much fuss. Since he couldn't sleep, he spent the time watching TV on my laptop in the treehouse. He couldn't change channels, so I just set it on the Super Scary Channel. We figured he might get some ideas about his situation.

We figured wrong.

"How can a ghost get scared?" I asked the next morning.

"I don't know," said Grimm. "I'm still me. Or mostly me. And I used to get scared. I guess I still get scared."

"You realize you're the lamest ghost ever, right?"

"Compared to whom? You know a lot of ghosts, do you?"

"Just the one," I said.

"Maybe we're all like this," said Grimm. "Maybe we're all regular people with regular fears—except, you know, dead-er-er."

"Dead-er-er is not a word."

"Alive-less-like."

"Again, not a word."

SUPERCREEPYLICIOUS!

"I'll allow it," I said as I stared at the Totally To-Do List on the wall of the treehouse. "Now what should we try next?"

"Swap identities for the day!"

"How exactly would that work?"

"You play dead and I'll pretend I'm alive."

"So, I'll go around all day whining about how bored I am with being dead, and you . . ."

". . . will go around all day acting all nervous and weird because I'm afraid I might sneeze the first time I kiss a girl."

"I don't worry about that."

"A real nasty sneeze. One of those stringy, snotty ones. But with chunks."

"Well, *now* I'm worried!"

"Let's pick another one."

"Yes. Let's."

Grimm suggested, "Biggest water balloon fight ever."

I nodded. "We can do that."

And we did.

Then we tried, "Adopt a pet."

After that we went with, "Hug a sloth." It just so happened that our neighbor Mrs. Meeley had a pet sloth. I don't know why. She just did. She was weird like that. She was also into competitive duck herding.

Maybe there was a connection.

Strike three and we were out.

CHAPTER 8

The next day was Monday. My first day back at school since Grimm died. No big deal. Except for the fact that he was hovering by my side.

You know, just another day.

Grimm and I attend Harriet Tubman Middle School. I mean, Grimm doesn't attend anymore. But I still do. It's a pretty cool school. You know, for a school. It's got all the normal school stuff . . . a gym, a cafeteria, a library, cool kids, normal kids, weird kids, and a freak or two.

DANNY DIGGER

WORE THE SAME SOCKS FOR THREE WEEKS

GOTHAR GRUBBER

CAN EAT A WHOLE BANANA BREAD IN ONE BITE.

Our mascot is a kraken.

You have to admit a kraken is a pretty cool mascot. It's scary. It has tentacles. And it comes out of nowhere to DESTROY you.

I tended to do okay in school. Good, not great grades. I kept to myself mostly. I tried to keep a low profile. Like I said earlier, I tried to blend in.

Which was hard when Grimm was around. Grimm never did blend.

But now? Now everything was different. Now I was on my own. And I was no longer invisible. Everyone was staring at me. I was sure they were all thinking, "There goes the dead kid's friend. Sucks to be him." Imagine what they'd have thought if they could see that Grimm was still around.

"We should start easy," added Grimm as we got off the bus. "You know, like climb the rope in gym."

"C'mon, that's never going to happen."

"Wait. How about 'talk to every kid in school'?"

"Every kid?"

"Every kid you run into."

"Can I just say 'Hey'?"

"No. At least one complete sentence."

"Who makes these rules?"

"I do! I can't do much, but I can make up rules."

"That makes no sense."

"What part of this makes ANY SENSE?!"

They never tell you how, when you have a ghost friend, you'll have to do everything yourself. There should be some sort of orientation. Right?

We entered the school. Kids everywhere. May as well get started.

First up was Mikey Hoover. What can I say about Mikey Hoover?

"See? This is easy!" whispered Grimm.

"Quiet!" I hissed.

Next up was Greta Bonobo. Greta was known for her great fashion sense. I'm not sure why.

"This is going great!" whispered Grimm.

"You're still here," I pointed out.

"You're just getting started," said Grimm.

Our next victim was Norman Witty. Who was not in any way witty. Or clean.

"I thought it looked like a squid," said Grimm.

"And . . . you're still here," I said again. "This isn't working."

"Patience," said Grimm. "God does not play dice with the universe."

I stared at Grimm. "What does that even mean?"

Grimm shrugged. "I don't know. But it sounded like a good thing to say."

"I'm going to Homeroom," I said.

I turned to leave when the absolute worst/best thing that could happen, happened (other than your best friend coming back as a ghost). Christi Mathison appeared.

"No," said Grimm. "You have to talk to her. Maybe *this* is what'll make the difference."

"That makes absolutely no sense. I'm doing the talking. Not you. This is about you. Not me."

"Who are you talking to, Larry?" asked Christi.

OKAY. BYE.

WHOOSH!

"Smooth," said Grimm.

"Oh, look who's *still* here," I said.

"There are four hundred kids at this school, and you've talked to four."

I stared at Grimm. He stared back. I sighed. We continued.

And of course, Grimm didn't budge from my side. Or from above me. Or from below me.

On our way to lunch, I pointed out the obvious. "You're really getting on my nerves."

"Gee, you think this is fun for me?" asked Grimm.

He was right. It's not like it was a contest, but Grimm's situation was worse. I mean, I was alive. Everyone was staring at me and feeling sorry for me, but I was alive. I felt bad.

I stopped in the hall and looked at Grimm. This meant to an outside observer I was staring at the bulletin board outside the office.

"I'm sorry," I said out loud.

"Larry, you should consider running," said an adult voice.

"Huh?" I said.

I turned. Ms. Spitzcracker, the principal, was smiling down at me.

"Running?" I said.

She pointed at the bulletin board.

"I don't know," I said.

"Right," said Grimm. "Like you could ever win student council president."

"Quiet," I whispered.

"Excuse me?" said Ms. Spitzcracker.

"Not you! I was just whispering out loud that I . . .

you know . . . shouldn't think or . . . um . . . whisper . . . out loud."

"Larry, are you okay?" asked Ms. Spitzcracker.

But I didn't say any of that. I just said, "I'm fine."

"Well, I know this is your first day back since Grimm passed. If you need anything at all . . . any help . . . anything . . . please don't hesitate to ask."

I didn't say that either.

Instead, I said, "Okay. Thanks."

Ms. Spitzcracker turned and walked into the office.

I stared at Grimm. "I *could* run. But I *choose* not to."

"It's just as well. If you won, then you'd be under a lot of pressure to name the auditorium after me."

"Pressure from who?"

"No one. I mean, no one alive."

CHAPTER 9

Lunch was tacos and tots. A popular lunch. But not as popular as pizza and tots. Or, you know . . . just tots.

I continued to try to talk to everybody. Word was starting to get around that I was acting weird.

"I'm not going to make it through all four hundred kids," I whispered to Grimm.

"No. I can see that," said Grimm. "I didn't anticipate how much you'd creep everyone out."

"Said the ghost kid only I can see."

"Maybe you need to talk to someone else. Someone different. Someone unique. Someone no one ordinarily talks to."

Grimm pointed across the cafeteria. I looked and there he was.

"No."

"Yes."

"No way."

"Yes way."

Boogie MacFarland was the class freak. He was raised by bears. Or maybe Bigfoot. Or maybe aliens.

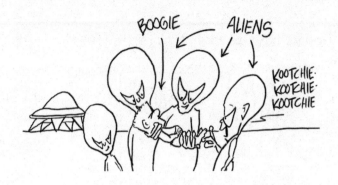

Boogie once knocked a kid out with a spit wad.

Boogie has webbed feet.

Boogie has a black belt in tongue fu.

It's like kung fu, but with more screaming.
He eats nails. Or staples. Or maybe it's paper clips.

Yes, Boogie was a bad dude. You gave Boogie a
wide berth. You didn't look at him, and you certainly
didn't talk to him.

"Go on, talk to him," said Grimm.

"Are you kidding? I'm not talking to Boogie."

"C'mon, what's the worst that could happen?"

THERE WILL BE TWO DEAD KIDS WITH NO IDEA HOW TO MOVE ON.

"He's harmless."

"Said the kid who can't be harmed anymore."

"But what if this is the thing? The thing that gets me to move on?"

"Why do all the *things* involve me risking my life?"

"No pain, no gain."

"My pain! Your gain!"

"Sure. Technically."

"You talk to him!"

"If I could, I would!"

Groan. No good options here. Dead if I do. Stuck with the dead if I don't.

I closed my eyes. I took a deep breath. I stood up and walked over to Boogie. He was hunched over the table. Writing something? His arms were covering it up.

I peered over his shoulder. Between his arms I could see a drawing. A really good drawing of a dragon. A zombie dragon.

"Cool," I said. "That's really good. You know, I like to draw too."

Boogie slowly turned his head toward me. I expected a look of annoyance. I expected a laser death stare. But what I got was . . . fear?

Boogie stood up. He started to back away from me. But his chair was in the way. What happened next happened in slow motion. Well, not really. But that's how I remembered it.

I poked my head up from under a pile of trays. Everything and everyone was covered in tacos and tots. Everyone, that is, except for one person.

HEY.

Yup. Still here.

CHAPTER 10

After what would become known as the Terrible Taco and Tot Fight of 2021, Boogie and I were sent to the office. I have never been sent to the office. I've seen kids get sent to the office. They don't come out the same.

"I don't belong here," I whispered at Grimm, who was hovering over the Bench of Shame.

"I've been here many times," said Grimm. "It's no big deal. The principal's just going to say how disappointed she is. She'll threaten to call your parents. Then she'll ask you . . .

. . . and then you'll get detention, and a . . .

"That's a thing?" I whispered.

"Oh yes," said Grimm. "Get enough marks and when you grow up, you can't vote or drive a car or watch R-rated movies."

"Really?" I asked.

"No! I'm kidding! There is no permanent record!"

"That's a relief."

"Are you okay?" asked Grimm.

I turned and stared at Grimm. I shook my head slowly. "No."

"Buddy, I need you to hang in there," said Grimm. "You're my only hope to get out of here."

"I don't know if I can help you," I said honestly.

"Are you talking to me?" asked Boogie from farther down the bench.

I whipped my head around. "No! I mean, yes . . . I mean . . . sort of."

"I don't want your help," said Boogie.

"Okay," I said.

"I don't want anybody's help."

"Sure."

Boogie was saying he didn't want anybody's help, but he didn't really look like he didn't want any help. He looked kind of sad. I felt bad for him. Maybe he just needed a friend.

"You weren't really raised by bears, were you?" I asked.

"What?" asked Boogie.

I said, "It's a thing around school. That you were raised by bears. And that you practice tongue fu. It's like kung fu but with more screaming. And you eat paper clips."

"Who told you that?" said Boogie.

"Well, nobody in particular. It's just what everyone says," I said.

"Everyone," agreed Grimm.

Boogie just shook his head like he'd heard it all before, but also like he couldn't do anything about it.

"I'm sorry your friend died," he said.

"What?" I said.

"Your friend, Grimm. I'm sorry he died."

"Thanks."

There was a beat of awkward silence.

"Did you know him?" I asked.

Boogie looked at me. "Everyone knew Grimm. He was . . . you know . . ."

"Grimm," I said.

I looked at Grimm. Then I looked at Boogie. Then for some reason, I got very sad all of a sudden. I could feel the tears coming, but I held them back. But they still welled up and went straight to my nose. I sniffed.

A little too loudly.

Boogie scooted over and put his hand on my shoulder. It was a heavy hand. But warm. I turned to him. He suddenly didn't look like a freak. He just looked like a kid. Sort of lost. Like the rest of us.

Ms. Spitzcracker leaned out of her office door. "Boogie, would you please come in?"

Boogie slowly rose, like he was fighting ten times the force of gravity. He walked up to Ms. Spitzcracker and said . . .

Ms. Spitzcracker stared at Boogie. I don't think she believed him. But she turned to me and said, "Larry, you can go."

I looked at Grimm. Grimm shrugged, and we left.

Out in the hall I said, "What just happened?"

"Boogie happened. He's just weird," said Grimm.

"Why did he take the fall?"

"He's the one that freaked out and started it."

"After I scared him."

"It's just Boogie. Who cares?"

"I do."

Grimm shrugged again.

I said, "I've always wondered where all that raised-by-bears, paper-clip stuff came from."

"Beats me," said Grimm. "Look, forget about Boogie—let's focus on me. What should we do next on the list?"

"*Someone* must have started it."

"Who *cares?*"

"I do," I said quietly. "It's not fair."

Grimm folded his arms. "Life isn't fair. And neither is death. It's time to move on."

"Fine," I said. "What's next on the list?"

"Feed Mr. Sniggles."

Mr. Sniggles was Mr. Vogal's dog next door. Mr. Sniggles was a peek-a-pit bull. Mr. Sniggles was evil.

"No way," I said. "That's dangerous."

"Come on," said Grimm. "We can do it!"

"We?" I asked.

"Well, you. But I'll be cheering you on," said Grimm. "You know, from the sidelines. Far, far away from the action."

I groaned.

"Hey, this is going to work. I can feel it. You feed Mr. Sniggles. I pass on."

"You promise?"

CHAPTER 11

The rest of the school day was uneventful, except for some unasked-for "help" from Grimm on a pop quiz.

It was sad to see that becoming a ghost hadn't made Grimm any smarter.

"I could have sworn it was Cabeza de Vaca," said Grimm later in the treehouse. "You know that Cabeza de Vaca means 'head of a cow' in Spanish, right?"

We laughed hard. Just like the old days. For a minute, everything was fine. Everything was normal. Everything was . . .

"This seems dangerous," I said, pointing out the obvious.

"He's a little dog. How much damage can he do?" said Grimm.

"Little dogs are the worst. They know they're small, so they bite big."

"Bite big?"

"Little dogs can unlock their jaws and take a massive bite out of you."

"Or so I've heard," I added.

Grimm said "Okay, so it might be a little dangerous. But maybe that's the thing. For me to move on, we have to do something hard. We have to show bravery."

"Again with the *we*."

Grimm stared at me. "You don't have to do it."

He's right. I didn't have to. I didn't owe Grimm anything. He was just a friend. A good friend. Who'd helped me come out of my shell.

Okay. I kind of owed him a lot.

Feeding a stupid tiny hellhound didn't seem that big a price to pay for all his friendship.

"What should I feed him?" I asked.

Grimm said, "I don't know. What do dogs like?"

"Twelve-year-old boys," I said with little doubt.

"A hot dog. Dog-eat-dog. Get it?"

I rolled my eyes. "Got it."

We climbed down from the treehouse. I retrieved a hot dog from the fridge and then proceeded to the back fence. I climbed up and peered over.

Mr. Sniggles was guarding a portal to the underworld.

Or maybe it was a pergola.

"He looks harmless," said Grimm. "This is going to be easy."

"For you," I said.

I climbed over the fence. Mr. Sniggles watched. He didn't growl. He didn't rush me. He just watched. I waved the hot dog in front of me.

"Hey, Mr. Sniggles," I called. "Look what I have."

Mr. Sniggles wasn't interested. He lay down and started licking himself.

I turned back to Grimm, who was watching from over the fence.

"I don't think he likes hot dogs," I said.

Grimm said, "Get closer."

I turned around.

I really shouldn't have turned around. If I hadn't turned around, I wouldn't have been face-to-face with Mr. Sniggles—and exposed to his breath.

Mr. Sniggles clearly ate poop. For breakfast, lunch and dinner. It was poop, poop, poop, with a side of poop.

I pushed Mr. Sniggles off me. I threw the hot dog at him, turned, and ran. Straight into a pool.

Did I mention that I can't swim? No? Well, I can't swim. Never got around to learning. Not sure why. Maybe it was because I've always been SCARED OF THE WATER!!

I'm pretty sure when you look in the Friendship Manual, there isn't anything about drowning for your dead friend so he can pass on to the next life.

Nope. Didn't think so.

Grimm tried to help. Which is to say, he didn't, or couldn't, help at all.

Panic set in. A wave of dread washed over me as I flailed in the water. I tried to scream for help, but my screams kept getting drowned out as my head went under. Eventually, my vision started to narrow.

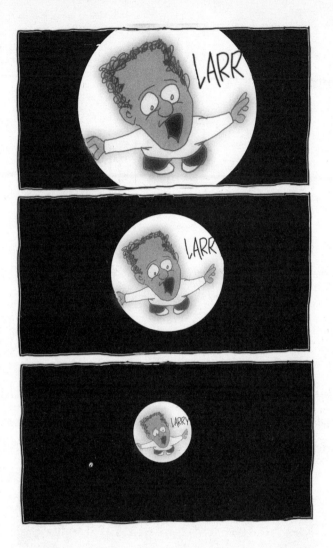

Just as I was about to black out and go under for the last time, I heard a howl. An animal howl. It was loud and guttural. It was the cat. It was the sound of the cat throwing up the mother of all hairballs.

That cat barfed so loud and so long that he alerted the whole neighborhood.

Including, thankfully, my mom.

Just as I went under, I heard my mom shriek, "Larry!"

Then I blacked out. The world went away, and I was floating in nothingness. The afterlife? It was dark, but warm. The panic and the fear were gone, replaced by . . . what? Anticipation? Anticipation of what would come next. What *would* come next? A light?

Nah, come on, too cliché.

"There's no light," said Grimm. "If there were, I'd go to it."

"Grimm?" I said.

"Relax. It's not your time. You're going to be fine."

"I don't feel fine," I said. "I feel lost."

"Soon you will be found," said Grimm.

"Found—?"

That's when I felt myself yanked back to life.

I was alive. I was throwing up water, and the tacos and tots I had for lunch. I looked up. My mom, soaking wet, was looking down at me. Grimm was floating behind her. The cat lay licking its paws nearby.

"You scared me," she said.

"Sorry," I said.

"We're done fooling around. You're going to see Dr. Hank *now*."

"Now?"

"Now!"

"Okay."

She put her arms around me and led me back into our yard. Grimm followed.

"Almost lost you, buddy," said Grimm.

"The cat," I whispered.

"Yeah, the cat saved your life."

"We should probably name it now."

"Yeah. Life-saving cats should have names."

"Hurl," I said.

"What?" said my mom.

I said, "The cat's name is Hurl."

Mom said, "You're in shock."

"Hurl," said Grimm.

CHAPTER 12

"What brings you here this evening, Larry?" said Dr. Hank.

I said, "I almost drowned."

"Oh, my."

"I was saved by the sound of a cat throwing up, which alerted my mom. We named the cat Hurl."

"Seems like a good name. Isn't that the same cat that your friend Grimm saved when he died?"

"Yeah."

"Grimm saves the cat. Then the cat saves you."

WEIRD, HUH?

"No. Just, you know, interesting," said Dr. Hank. "What were you doing in the pool?"

I said, "I was trying to feed Mr. Sniggles a hot dog when he jumped on me. I ran away from him and into the pool."

"Even though you can't swim."

"I didn't have a lot of time to think about it."

"Why were you feeding Mr. Sniggles?"

"It's on the list."

"What list?"

"The Totally To-Do List from the treehouse. Grimm and I made it."

"A bucket list?"

"What?"

"A list of things to do before you die."

"I guess. But we didn't make it because we thought anyone was going to die."

"Of course not. So, you've been doing stuff from the list."

"Yeah."

"Why?"

What do I say? The truth? Seems like a bad idea. They might lock me up. Do they do that? Maybe they just give me a bunch of pills. Maybe the pills will make Grimm go away. But would he really go away? Or would I just think he went away?

A lot of questions. No answers.

I said, "It's for Grimm. He couldn't complete the list, but I can."

"That's very thoughtful," said Dr. Hank. "Dangerous, but thoughtful. You must really miss Grimm."

"Yeah. He's a good friend."

"He was a good friend."

"Right. Was."

Dr. Hank looked at me for a few seconds. He looked like he was trying to read my mind. Could he do that? Were therapists mind readers? I was only twelve. There was a lot of stuff I didn't know.

STUFF I DON'T KNOW
1. THE CAPITAL OF LATVIA.
2. WHO INVENTED CHEESE?
3. WHERE MY SPLEEN IS.
4. HOW TO KISS A GIRL.

Dr. Hank said, "Is Grimm with us now?"

"No!"

I mean, he'd wanted to be here, but I had said no way.

Way too weird.

Dr. Hank said, "You know, it's okay if you see him. It's perfectly normal to think you see a close friend who just died."

I said, "I'm not seeing Grimm."

At least, not right now.

"Your mom told me you've been talking to yourself a lot."

"I guess."

"Does anyone talk back?"

Grimm is a chatterbox.

SO I DIED. THEN I WAS A GHOST. AND I THOUGHT "COOL." BUT IT'S PRETTY BORING AND AND I CAN'T PEE. I LIKE TO PEE.

YAWN

"No," I said.

"Okay," said Dr. Hank. "Good. That's good."

That's when Dr. Hank did something that threw me. He hunched forward and looked me straight in the eye.

There's this thing that happens with me and adults. I guess I don't expect them to understand, and when they do it surprises me. It surprises me a lot.

I said, "It's . . . it's just hard."

"I know," said Dr. Hank. "It's the finality of it all.

Grimm was here. Now he's gone. But his presence persists. You feel like he's still here."

"Yes."

"But he isn't."

"Yes. I mean, no. Wait. I mean, yes."

Dr. Hank gave me a box of tissues. I dabbed my eyes and blew my nose. I felt better. Maybe I really was seeing things. Maybe I just wanted Grimm to be here. Maybe . . .

"Dude?" said a familiar voice.

I looked up.

"You're not here," I said out loud.

"What?" said Grimm.

"What?" asked Dr. Hank.

Dr. Hank looked at me. He glanced at the window. Then back at me. I was ready for him to break out the pills.

But he didn't.

"Larry, you're going to be okay. You know how I know that? Because a lot of people care about you. We'll talk about this more next week."

I turned to leave. I took one more look at Grimm in the window.

CHAPTER 13

"Hey man, what happened?" said Grimm as he followed me out of Dr. Hank's office.

I ignored him as I joined my mom in the waiting room.

"Everything okay?" asked Mom.

I nodded.

Dr. Hank was behind me. "He's fine. I'll see him next week."

"Okay," said Mom. "Larry, why don't you go outside to the car? I'll be out in a minute."

"Larry?" asked Grimm.

EVERYTHING COOL?

I didn't say anything. I left the office and went outside. Grimm followed.

I sat on the hood of our car and waited for Mom.

"What did he do to you, Larry?" asked Grimm. "Did he roboticize you?"

"Lobotomize," I said.

"Awesome! Did it tickle?"

"He didn't lobotomize me. All he said was . . ."

"What?"

"Never mind."

"What did he say?"

"He said . . ."

"WHAT?"

"But I am real. You can see me. You can talk to me."

I stared at Grimm. "None of this is real."

"Larry?"

"I embarrassed myself at school. I was sent to the office. I almost drowned. None of that is me. Something's wrong with me. And that something is . . ."

"You're not real!" I said again.

Grimm backed away. "Larry!"

"Larry, stop!" yelled Grimm.

I collapsed on the ground. I looked up and saw my reflection in the office window.

"Larry, I am real!"

I pointed to the window.

GRIMM!

CHAPTER 14

"What is wrong with me?" I said out loud.

MEOW.

"Really not helpful," I said.

Hurl shrugged, then slowly trotted to the corner of the treehouse and curled up.

I was alone.

Wait.

Yup. all alone. By myself. Solitary. Lonely. So, so lonely.

I already lost my best friend once.

Now I'd lost him again!

Look, I hadn't meant to lose Grimm. It was just not easy having a dead friend around . . . for *lots* of reasons.

REASONS IT'S HARD TO HAVE A DEAD FRIEND

1. THEY'RE DEAD.
2. THEY'RE DEAD.
3. THEY'RE DEAD.
4. AND THEY'RE STILL DEAD.

Still, I felt bad that I'd told him he wasn't real. Which was true. But also false. He would always be real to me. Whether he was a ghost or not.

I wished there was some way I could apologize. How do you apologize to a ghost? A séance? Wait. Didn't we have a Ouija board?

WE DO!

I threw the board together and put my fingers on the guide.

"Grimm, I'm sorry."

Nothing.

Maybe I needed four hands. Or two hands and two paws.

Still nothing. Wait. It started moving.

Again, not helping, cat.

What else could I do? I looked around the tree-house. All I could see was a bunch of beat-up board games and an old mirror. Wait! A mirror. What was that thing again? Say "Bloody Mary" three times, and she appears? What if . . .

I shook my head. "You're disgusting."

"Meow," said Hurl.

Was Grimm really gone? Could he have passed on? I didn't think so. Felt like he was still out there somewhere.

Waiting.

Waiting to move on?

I went to the treehouse window to investigate. It wasn't Grimm. It was Mr. Sniggles, staring up at me from the neighbor's yard.

"Stupid dog," I said out loud.

"Meow," agreed Hurl.

Mr. Sniggles stared. Like he was daring me. Daring me to feed him a hot dog and prove I wasn't afraid. It was like he was saying . . .

Which was really stupid. How was feeding a hot dog to a dumb dog proof that I was brave? That was exactly the kind of thing that Grimm would think.

Wait. That's exactly the kind of thing Grimm had said!

FOR ME TO
MOVE ON WE
HAVE TO DO
SOMETHING
HARD...
SOMETHING
BRAVE.

Maybe this was what Grimm needed to move on. I mean, I wanted him to come back, but maybe that wasn't what he really needed now. Maybe this was what he was out there waiting for. Maybe it really was the list. Maybe I had to complete this thing, not just because it was hard, but because it was the hardest thing on the list. Harder even than kissing a girl. At least, I hoped so.

I'VE GOT TO DO THIS!

Wait. One more thing, just in case.

CHAPTER 15

Mr. Sniggles growled. It was one of those upturned-lip, show-him-your-teeth growls. It was an I'm-going-to-eat-your-spleen growl. It was a giant flashing neon sign to that little guy in my brain that processes danger.

No. I needed to do this. I really needed to do this.

Wait. Why did I need to do this again? Oh, right. To help Grimm to move on by being brave. Wait. Does that make sense?

"Show no fear," said Grimm from behind me.

Hey, it worked! Grimm was back. Now I didn't have to risk my life.

Too late.

"Relax," said Grimm. "You're fine. Just ask yourself, what would Grimm do in this situation?"

"I don't know," I said. "Say 'Boo'?"

"No! When I was alive. What would I do?"

Well, that wasn't an easy question. Grimm responded in a lot of different ways when faced with a scary situation.

Grimm was unpredictable. There was no way to know which way . . .

That's when I knew exactly what to do. There was really only one thing to do. And that was . . . EVERY-THING!

My work here was done.

CHAPTER 16

"Way to stand up to Mr. Sniggles. That was impressive," said Grimm.

"It was, wasn't it?" I said.

We were back in the treehouse. Grimm was back to his floating, ghostly self.

"I'm really sorry about what happened," I said. "I didn't mean to say you're not real."

Grimm said, "Don't worry about it. I'm not as real as I used to be, but I'm not *not* real."

"You're real-ish."

LIFE-LITE.

I LIKE IT!

"Where did you go?" I asked.

"I hung out at the park for a while. Then I went to the mall. Then I watched those raccoons. It's really lonely being a ghost."

"So, that's why you came back?"

"That, and I figured you might try to do something stupid."

"Or brave."

"Kind of the same thing."

"You're back, which is cool. But you're still here, which is not cool. Now what?"

"Unfinished business," said Grimm. "Remember?"

"Right. You want to go back to the Totally To-Do List?"

"No. That doesn't seem to be working."

"Yeah. I thought Mr. Sniggles would do the trick, but no. Now what?"

"I'm not sure. I think whatever we do needs to make some sort of difference."

"What kind of difference?"

"Something I should have done while I was alive.

Or someone I should have helped. Or someone I should have . . . or someone I need to . . ."

"There was that time you were supposed to help me with my science project. You know, the nuclear reactor made out of popsicle sticks."

"I provided the sticks."

"By eating all the popsicles."

"That's HELPING!"

"It wasn't helping me."

"Wait," said Grimm. "That's it."

"What's it?" I asked.

"It's just like with Mr. Sniggles!"

"I'm not following."

"I need to help you . . ."

"You're dead," I pointed out.

"No. Not me NOW. Me THEN! I need to help you be like me. . . ."

"Wait," I said. "So you think you're still here to help me go on without you?"

"It makes perfect sense!" said Grimm.

"None of this makes perfect sense."

"You know what I mean."

"But I like having you around."

"And I like hanging with you. But I don't like that you're the only one I can talk to. And I don't like that I can't interact with anyone. And I really, really miss peeing."

"I guess I understand," I said. "Not the peeing part, but the other parts."

"This has to be it! This has to be my unfinished business! I need to save you from being you, so you can be like me! And then survive without me!"

It was true that me, as Larry, was—you know—a work in progress. I was quiet, shy, and prone to worry. It might be nice to be less quiet, less shy, and a bit more confident.

"But I'm not kissing any girls."

"Aren't you a little curious?"

"Fine. Fine. We'll work up to that."

"You are a very annoying ghost."

CHAPTER 17

"First thing we do is fix your . . . um . . . look," said Grimm.

I said, "I look fine."

We were in the restroom at school just before the first bell.

Grimm continued, "I want you looking exactly like me."

"I can't be black," I said.

"Sadly, no. But I can teach you everything I know about style and fashion."

"You know almost nothing about style and fashion."

"Which is infinitely more than you."

This was true. My mom handled all the fashion.

"Let's see what we can do," said Grimm.

The restroom door opened. Boogie entered.

"Hey," I said.

"Hey," said Boogie.

We all just stood there.

"Thank you for what you did the other day," I said.

"She didn't believe me," said Boogie, looking disappointed.

"Are you okay?" I asked.

Boogie looked a bit shocked at the question. Like no one had ever asked him if he was okay before.

"Um . . . yeah," muttered Boogie.

"Good," I said.

We stood there for a second, not saying anything again.

"So, you draw any more dragons?"

"What?"

"Dragons. Before the food fight broke out, you were drawing dragons."

"Oh. No. No dragons."

He fumbled in his pocket, pulled out a piece of paper, and handed it to me.

"Cool!" I said.

"I have a little trouble with the brains dripping out of his head. It looks too much like Jell-O."

"Oh, that's easy to fix. See, you just add a little shading and some texture. I can show you sometime."

"This is SO boring!" cried Grimm.

"Please be quiet," I said under my breath.

"What?" said Boogie.

"Not you. I was just talking to—"

Boogie stared at me. He looked a little scared.

"I gotta go," he said.

And he left. I looked at Grimm and frowned.

I said, "Please stop talking to me when I'm talking to someone who's alive."

"It's just Boogie," said Grimm.

I looked at the drawing again and shoved it in my pocket. "You made me scare him off before he could use the restroom."

"He was never going to go with us in here," said Grimm. "Shy bladder."

"You don't know that."

"When you're raised by bears there's lots of time and room to go in the woods. You get used to being by yourself."

"You made that up."

"It's true."

"It's not."

"Who cares?" said Grimm. "This is about me making you more like me, so that I can pass on!"

"Right," I said.

But I couldn't focus. I kept thinking about Boogie. Something was off with that guy. Something more than only being comfortable peeing in the woods.

"Clearly, we can't do anything about your look," said Grimm, "but we can work on your attitude. Turn around and face the mirror. Repeat after me."

CHAPTER 18

"I want you to say everything I tell you to say," said Grimm as we walked/floated down the hall to class.

"Here comes Mikey Greenwald," said Grimm. "Tell him he looks like he gets his hair cut by bees."

I said, "I'm not going to say that. It's mean."

"He'll love it. We kid each other all the time like that."

"You're sure?"

"Of course I'm sure."

Grimm laughed. "Ha ha! That was great!"

I said, "No it wasn't. He was crying!"

"He always cries. That's what makes it funny!"

"It's not funny!"

"I don't know. Everyone else thinks it's funny."

"People love you!" said Grimm. "Well actually, they loved me, but now with my help they'll love you and you won't need me and I'll get to move on."

"You're still here."

"You can't achieve full Grimm-ness all at once. It takes time. You'll get there. Be patient."

This didn't feel right. Whatever *unfinished business* Grimm had, it wasn't about making me into a jerk.

"Hey, here comes Christi. Just do everything I tell you."

I said, "No, Grimm."

But it was too late.

"You didn't say anything I told you to say," cried Grimm.

I smiled. "I know."

"You completely blew it with her!"

"I don't think so."

"She's never going to kiss us now!"

"Us?"

"You know what I mean."

"Look Grimm . . . I don't think that . . ."

"I'm doing the best I can. I've never been a ghost before. It's all new. It's all weird. It's all . . ."

"Hey, it's okay," I said.

"But you're not trying to be me," said Grimm.

"Maybe this isn't about me being *you* so I can be without you," I said. "Maybe this is about me being *me* so I can be without you."

"I don't understand."

"I can't be you."

"Well, obviously. That would involve a wet cat and a violent thunderstorm."

I said, "But I can be me."

"But you're invisible. I know invisible. I'm a ghost," said Grimm. "Look, you don't need to *be* me. You need to be more *like* me. More Grimm-ish. Less Larry-ish.

Don't you get it? I really, really need you to get it!"

I was pretty sure Grimm was wrong, but I could see his growing desperation. The ghost thing was getting old, and he clearly needed to get out of here. If I could help him, I needed to try.

"I get it," I said. "Also, Tangerine and Lava Axe body spray makes me break out in hives."

Grimm smiled. "Noted. Now, let's get your Grimm on!"

CHAPTER 19

Despite my doubts, I made a good-faith effort to spend the rest of the school day trying to channel my inner Grimm.

He says "ta-da" ALL the time.

Basically, it was a lot of accidentally doing stupid stuff and then pretending you meant to do the stupid stuff on purpose.

It wasn't all silly/stupid stuff, pretending to be Grimm. He had some good qualities I could emulate.

Finally, the school day was over. As we walked to the bus, I realized I was only a little more like Grimm at the end of the day than I had been at the beginning.

"You didn't do most of things I said to do!" said Grimm.

I said, "I did the best I could. But this isn't work-ing."

"You're not trying hard enough."

"I'm trying as hard as I can!" I whispered loudly.

Grimm said, "I'm never getting out of here."

I took a deep breath. "Let's get on the bus, go home, and figure this out."

Just as we were about to get on the bus, we heard a commotion behind us. We turned around to the sight of Boogie being harassed by a bunch of girls.

"We should do something," I said.

Grimm said, "Why? It's just Boogie."

"He needs help."

"Dude, he started shaving at six!"

Grimm shook his head. "He doesn't need our help."

"I don't care," I said. "I'm going to help him."

I put my backpack down and marched over to Boogie and the girls.

"Well," I said, "you're being mean."

The first girl said, "It's just Boogie."

"I know," I said, "but why are you angry at him?"

This question was met with silence and looks of confusion.

"Everyone teases Boogie," said the second girl.

"It's a thing," said the third girl.

Boogie shrugged. "It really is kind of a thing,"

"Seriously, it's a thing," whispered Grimm in my ear.

"It's not a *thing!*" I yelled it loudly enough for everyone in the general vicinity to hear, stop what they were doing, and turn and stare at me.

179

"It's not *this* big of a thing," whispered Grimm.

"Will you stop!" I said.

"Who are you talking to?" asked the first girl.

Now, this was about the twenty-eighth time I'd been caught talking to myself/Grimm. I was getting tired of explaining. Was it time to tell the truth?

"I'm talking to Grimm! You know, my friend? Who died? He's floating right here! He's a ghost! And if you don't leave Boogie alone . . ."

There was silence. And not the good kind of silence. Not the kind of silence when your mom smiles after seeing you actually rinse your dishes and put them in the dishwasher after being asked only three times.

No, it was the kind of silence like when your dad's

younger brother Devon who never really made anything of himself says he's going to clown college, and there's nothing anyone in his family can say to talk him out of it.

Anyway, back to the truth-telling silence.

"No! I'm not okay! I'm really sick and tired of ev-eryone asking me if I'm okay! But I'm really, REALLY sick and tired of everyone picking on Boogie!"

"It's just Boogie," said the first girl again.

"You know he was raised by bears, right?" said the second girl.

"And he eats paper clips," said the third girl.

I turned to Boogie. "Boogie, do you eat paper clips?"

"No," said Boogie. "I do like Fig Newtons."

"Were you raised by bears?" I asked.

"No. I saw a bear in a zoo once. He waved to me."

I turned back to the girls. "Where do you get this stuff?"

They stopped and looked at each other.

"Should we tell him?" said the first girl.

"I don't want to tell him. You tell him," said the second girl.

"I'm not going to tell him," said the third girl.

GRIMM TOLD THEM.

I turned around to stare at Grimm. Who, as you know, only I could see, so it looked like I was talking to a bike rack.

"I'm not laughing!" I screamed.

When kids talk about this day (and they do talk about it (ALL THE TIME!)), they say that it looked like I was strangling a ghost. Which *is* actually what I was doing.

"Boogie?" said Grimm.

"Boogie," I said.

"You're right," said Grimm. "Oh my god, you're right. I'm so sorry."

"Larry?" said a familiar voice.

I turned. It was Ms. Spitzcracker. She was staring down at me with a look of deep concern.

"Oh . . . hi, Ms. Spitzcracker," I said.

"Larry, I think you should come with me."

"Where are we going?" I asked.

CHAPTER 20

"What's new?" asked Dr. Hank.

"Not much," I said.

"Hmm . . . I don't think that's true."

"What do you want me say?"

"You could start with the truth."

Right.

Yeah, that was not going to work.

"A thing happened at school," I said.

Dr. Hank asked, "A thing?"

"There was this kid, Boogie. He was being picked on. And I tried to help him. Stuff happened."

"Stuff?"

"I got upset. I said some things."

"More things?"

"I might have said something about Grimm. About how he's a ghost. And I talk to him."

"Huh."

"I don't really talk to him. I talk to myself. But people think I'm talking to him. But I'm not. That would be weird. That would be crazy."

"No. Not crazy."

"Pretty sure it's crazy."

"Larry, we talked about this last time. It's perfectly normal to grieve for your friend. But everyone grieves differently. For you, grieving means talking to—"

"—Myself."

"—Grimm."

"I'm not talking to Grimm," I said.

Dr. Hank smiled. "It's okay. People talk to dead people all the time."

"No, they don't."

"My mother passed away a few years ago. I talk to her all the time."

"And she talks back?"

"And back. And back. And back. She's a real chatterbox."

"But not really."

"Our minds are amazing things. When we're anxious or worried or sad or grieving, our minds sometimes come to the rescue by bringing our loved ones back for a quick chat."

"But it's not real."

"No, it's not real. But it feels real. It feels real to me. Does it feel real to you?"

I turned and looked out the window.

"Tell me more about this Boogie character," said Dr. Hank.

"He's this big, older kid at school that everyone picks on," I said.

"Why?"

SOMEONE TOLD A BUNCH OF LIES ABOUT HIM.

"Hmm . . . could that someone be Grimm?"

"How'd you know?"

"A hunch. Sounds like maybe your issues might have something to do with guilt."

"Not my guilt. I didn't make stuff up about Boogie."

"But you believed it. And you teased Boogie, too."

"I guess."

"Maybe now that Grimm is gone you've taken on some of his guilt. But maybe you have some of your own guilt too?"

"Maybe."

"Maybe, just maybe, if you help Boogie you're helping Grimm. And yourself."

"Helping Grimm how?"

"Move on."

"Move on where?"

"Wherever *you* need him to go."

I could think of a lot of places I'd like Grimm to go.

PLACES WHERE GRIMM CAN GO

1. FAR, FAR AWAY FROM ME.
2. THE PLACE FARTHER AWAY FROM THE FAR, FAR AWAY PLACE.
3. MARS.

"I want him to go wherever he wants to go."

"So, maybe you figure out a way to help this Boogie," said Dr. Hank.

"He's really unpopular," I said.

"That's just because no one knows the real Boogie. They just know the Boogie that Grimm made up."

"Grimm said he was raised by bears."

"Yes, he set a high bar to get over."

"And he eats paper clips."

"Higher still."

"And he seems pretty used to being picked on."

"How about you just start by being his friend?"

"Then everyone will make fun of me."

"Or . . . they'll say, 'There's cool Larry with Boogie. Maybe Boogie is cool too.'"

"Give it a shot," said Dr. Hank. "In memory of Grimm. What do you say?"

It made sense. Grimm should be into it. It may be his only way out. And mine. After all, I was guilty of teasing Boogie too. I turned to look for Grimm. But he was gone.

CHAPTER 21

I found Grimm in the treehouse with Hurl.

"You left Dr. Hank's," I said.

"I didn't like being described as a figment of your imagination."

"You're not. In my imagination, your butt is much bigger."

"You know, he could be right."

"So, I'm hallucinating?"

"It's possible."

"What's my favorite food?"

"Mac and cheese."

"How many times have I been the last man standing in Fortnight?"

"None. You're terrible at building shelters. Skylights? I always blast you through the skylight!"

"And who did I have a secret crush on last year?"

Grimm paused. He looked around.

"I don't know."

"Exactly. But I do. And if you were a hallucination, you would know too. So, you're real."

"Also," I continued, "if you were a hallucination, you'd know this: what are we going to do next?"

"I have no idea," said Grimm.

"We make Boogie popular," I said.

"How?"

"We have to change his image. We have to change the image you gave him."

"But how?"

I wasn't sure. At this point, all I had were a few bad ideas.

BAD IDEAS

1. CHANGE HIS NAME TO THOR.
2. START A RUMOR HE'S FROM FRANCE.
3. HAVE HIM TAKE A SHOWER WITH TANGERINE AND LAVA AXE BODY SPRAY.
4. TEACH HIM TO POP AND LOCK.

"Those are bad ideas," said Grimm.

"Yes, they are," I agreed.

"This isn't going to work. It's impossible."

"You don't know that."

"I'm going to be stuck here forever."

"No, you're not."

"What am I going to do?"

Again, I wasn't sure. But I had some ideas.

THINGS GRIMM CAN DO

1. SCARE KIDS AT BIRTHDAY PARTIES.
2. WALK THROUGH WALLS JUST BECAUSE HE CAN.
3. NEVER HAVE TO TAKE A BATHROOM BREAK AT MOVIES.

"Or what if it does work?"

"Then you pass on."

"Where?"

"Heaven, I guess."

"I hear in heaven they have no root beer. That's why we drink it here."

"I'm sure there's root beer in heaven."

"You don't know. It could be this big, boring place

where everyone is perfect, and everyone says nice things to each other, and nobody ever takes a bath in spaghetti."

"I'm sure spaghetti baths are allowed."

"None of the popular depictions I've seen feature them. There's a lot of harps and clouds and gates, but no spaghetti baths."

"You're being silly."

I didn't know what to say. What do you say to your dead best friend who's freaking out about spaghetti baths in heaven? They never covered this in health class.

"I know you're scared. And I'm sorry. I'm sorry you're dead. I'm sorry you're a ghost. I'm sorry you made up all that stuff about Boogie. And I'm sorry I believed you and teased him, too. But I think our best bet for you to move on is to try and help Boogie. You said yourself that it had to be something you NEED to fix. Actually, whether you move on or not, you still need to fix this."

"Who died and elected you King of Making Sense?"

"Wait. That's it! The election!"

"Isn't that in like a week?"

"Yes. We have our work cut out for us."

"Maybe we should just go back to 'Kiss a girl.'"

"No! We're going to run Boogie for student council president and he's going to win and you're going to heaven to take all the spaghetti baths you want!"

"One big happy ending."

"Or I'll die trying."

CHAPTER 22

This was the first time since Grimm came back that I really thought we were onto something. I had a good feeling about all this. I just knew that by making Boogie into the most popular kid at school, Grimm could pass on.

There was just one problem.

How do you make the most unpopular kid in school the most popular kid in school?

"He has to have some redeeming qualities," said Grimm.

"He's large," I pointed out.

"True. But size in and of itself does not make a kid popular."

It was the next day at lunch at school. I was sitting by myself, because now I was the weird kid who talked to himself.

"Was King Kong popular?" I asked.

"Well, sort of. I guess," said Grimm. "But Boogie is not exceptionally large. He's just regular large."

"I guess that would be true for Godzilla as well."

"Yes. And Mothra."

"Hmm."

"I'll bet Boogie is strong."

"Yes. That would stand to reason."

"What if, like, a bus fell on someone and Boogie lifted it off? That would make him popular."

"Who's going to volunteer to have a bus fall on them?" asked Grimm.

"Not me," I said.

"Not anybody."

"C'mon, there's got to be something we can work with. Let's make a list. Do you have a piece of paper?"

"I'm a ghost."

I rolled my eyes and pulled off my backpack. I unzipped it and grabbed the first piece of paper I could find.

"What is it?" asked Grimm.

"It's Boogie's artwork," I said. "From the restroom. I must have put it in my backpack."

"Boogie can draw?"

"Yeah. And he's really good."

"Hmm."

"'Hmm' what?"

"You can draw too."

"So?"

"I've got an idea."

CHAPTER 23

"Wait. Tag the school?" I asked.

"That's my idea!" said Grimm. "Both you and Boogie are great at drawing. You tag the school and we'll give Boogie all the credit."

"Isn't graffiti, like, vandalism? That's a real crime. You know, where they put you in real jail with real criminals like loiterers and jay-walkers and people who throw gum on the sidewalk."

"Gum on the sidewalk?"

"The worst!"

"We'll use non-permanent spray chalk."

"Is that a thing?"

"Yeah. I've used it before."

"Wait. So *you* were the one who tagged the boys' bathroom last year."

Grimm smiled. "Can't catch me now."

"Okay," I said. "One other problem. How do we give Boogie the credit without him knowing or anyone else knowing? I can't sign the tags with his name. He'll get in trouble."

"Hmm . . . I don't know. But we'll figure it out. Meanwhile, let's come up with some ideas for cool drawings."

"How about something like this?"

"Maybe something a bit more specific. More pro-active."

"You think?"

"Sure, it's a popular opinion, but is it a unique opinion?"

"How about this?"

"Much better."

"Meow," meowed Hurl.

CHAPTER 24

I raided my piggy bank to buy a bunch of spray chalk at the hardware store. The guy at the store was suspicious, but we gave him a good story.

We got to school and got to work. We tagged the boys' bathroom.

We tagged the boys' locker room.

And we snuck into a laundry hamper and tagged the girls' locker room, so it wouldn't be obvious it was a boy.

At lunch we tagged under the cafeteria tables.

Then we tagged a bunch of lockers when no one was around.

Word got around fast about the graffiti. Everyone wanted to know who was doing it. Pictures started showing up on ZippyGram.

That's when Grimm got an even better idea.

"What is it?" I said.

"I figured out how we're going to get everyone to know it was Boogie," he said.

"How?"

"Boogie's going to take credit."

"How."

"Boogie's going to become really popular on ZippyGram."

"I'm confused."

"It's simple. We make up a fake account for Boogie. Boom! We don't make it super obvious it's him. Boom! We somehow in a way I haven't thought of yet make it obvious to everyone that it's Boogie. Boom! Then everyone thinks he's cool. Boom! Then one of us suggests that everyone write him in for student council president. Boom!"

"You like saying, 'Boom.'"

"I don't know," I said. "A lot of things have to go just right for this to work."

Grimm said, "You're always so negative. Have a little faith. What could go wrong?"

The list of things that could go wrong was long and very, very scary.

THINGS THAT COULD GO
WRONG

1. ZOMBIES. JUST ZOMBIES.
2. WE GET CAUGHT 'CAUSE YOU KNOW, CSI STUFF.
3. MS. SPITZCRACKER IS PSYCHIC.
4. STUPID PLANS NEVER WORK.

CHAPTER 25

The next day at school everyone was abuzz about the graffiti.

We needed just one more tag to nail it down. Something big. Something awesome. Something viral.

"You should tag something right above the principal's door," said Grimm.

"That's crazy," I said.

"No. It's big. It's daring. It's bold."

"It's insane. I'll get caught."

"You can do this. You've grown. You've changed. You're not you anymore. You're Larry 2.0."

He was right. I had changed.

"How am I supposed to tag above the principal's door?"

"You use a ladder, or a box, or a chair, dummy."

"Which I could fall off of and break my arm, a really bad break where the bone sticks through, and it gets all infected and they have to amputate it and then everyone calls me 'Stumpy.'"

I wish I could say that tagging above the principal's door went smoothly, but after all that's happened, you would know I'd be lying.

Let's just say it went . . . somewhat *less* than smoothly.

BOUNCE!

AHHHHHH!

TH-THUMP!

"You did it!" cheered Grimm.

I nodded. "I did, didn't I."

"This whole me-dying thing has really brought you out of your shell."

"I'm going to miss you when you're gone," I said.

"Oh, I'm sure I'll always be around."

"You know, in an invisible sort of 'looking over you, but not really around you' sort of way."

"Can I at least go to the bathroom by myself?"

"Yes, I promise."

"Pinky swear."

PINKY SWEAR.

CHAPTER 26

That last tag got everyone talking. And by talking, I mean commenting on ZippyGram.

All that was needed was a little comment from yours truly to set everyone on a Boogie-for-president trajectory.

Grimm counted down, "Five, four, three . . ."

Grimm frowned. "I didn't even get to one."

It worked. Everyone was texting about Boogie being the mysterious tagger.

At this point, all it took was one anonymous comment that everyone write in Boogie for student council president!

And we were off.

Of course, Boogie had no idea any of this was going on. Although he *was* starting to get suspicious.

Boogie confronted us. I mean, me.

"What's going on?" asked Boogie.

"Play dumb," said Grimm.

"What're you talking about?" I said.

"You've done something."

"I do some things every day. I am a regular doer of things."

"Everyone is being nice to me. One girl winked at me. No girl has ever winked at me before."

"You're a good-looking dude."

"Please."

"Hey. You're large! And you shave. I won't be shaving for like five years. Girls dig older men."

"No. You've done something," said Boogie. "Something you think will help me. But I don't want to be helped."

"Okay," said Grimm. "Time to lie."

Sure. Lie. Of course. Except . . . I really was trying to help Boogie. And not just to help Grimm. Or fix what Grimm did. I really wanted Boogie to be popular. He deserved to be popular. Even though he didn't seem to want to be popular. Which was weird.

Boogie said, "You did the graffiti, didn't you?"

"Yes," I said.

"No!" yelled Grimm. "What are you doing?"

Boogie continued, "And you told everyone it was me."

"Yes."

"Why?"

"We . . . I mean, *I* was just trying to make you popular by running you for student council president. And then everyone can see who you really are."

"But I don't want to be student council president," said Boogie.

I said, "I just wanted you to be a normal and popular kid like, you know . . ."

"You?"

Grimm interrupted, "Dude, you're not that popular."

"Not me," I said. "But someone popular. Someone who's super confident. Someone who believes in themselves."

Boogie shook his head. "In other words, someone who *you* want to be."

"Well, who wouldn't want to be like that?"

ME.

I said, "What?"

Boogie explained, "When you're popular, kids want stuff from you. They want your popularity to rub off on them. They want your popularity to fill them with whatever they need. They want you to fix whatever is wrong with them. I don't want that. I don't need that.

It's too much pressure. I like to stick to myself. Even if that makes me unpopular."

Grimm and I stared at Boogie. He stared back. There was a look in Boogie's eyes. A look that shot straight through all the self-serving hooey I had been shoveling.

He was right.

I was wrong.

We were wrong.

"Boogie, could I speak to you in my office?" said Ms. Spitzcracker behind me.

"What?" asked Boogie.

Ms. Spitzcracker said, "It's about the recent graffiti around school."

Boogie didn't say anything. He just stared at me and then slowly followed Ms. Spitzcracker to her office.

"He's going to take the fall?" said Grimm.

I hesitated for just a second. I could have just stayed put. None of what was going to land on Boogie would bury me. I could just walk away. Who would blame me? It was just Boogie.

Wait. You know who would blame me?

I would blame me.

CHAPTER 27

It was a shame. It was such a good plan. We were doing a good thing to help a good person. There was just one problem. Boogie wasn't the one who needed help.

I was.

And, of course, Grimm.

"Don't do this," said Grimm.

I said, "I have to."

"You don't. We'll figure something out."

"There's nothing to figure out. It's over. Ms. Spitzcracker is going to expose the whole thing. Boogie won't be elected student council president."

Grimm shook his head. "I just wanted to undo the damage I did."

I nodded. "And I was just trying to help you."

That was the problem. We were trying to do the wrong thing for the right reasons. We were trying to help someone who didn't want or need our help.

"Are you going in?" asked Grimm.

I had an idea. Probably not a good idea. Probably a terrible idea. Probably the worst idea in the history of bad ideas. But . . . maybe not.

"I've got an idea," I said to Grimm.

"Does it involve graffiti, or a peek-a-pit bull, or spaghetti baths?"

"No. It involves the truth."

CHAPTER 28

You're probably wondering why I was standing in front of an assembly of the entire school. Well, so was I.

I told Ms. Spitzcracker the truth, the whole truth, and nothing but the truth, so help me Grimm.

I told Ms. Spitzcracker she could put me in detention for the rest of my life, but first I wanted to tell the whole school the truth. And I wanted to apologize.

Ms. Spitzcracker just sat there for a few moments and stared at me. It was a generous stare. Like she felt bad for me, but also like she was kind of proud of me. I was still in serious trouble. I had questioned the quality and edibility of the cafeteria food (except for the tots . . . the tots were tops). I had to pay with triple-double-extra-hard-time detention. No smartphones, no books, just stare at the ceiling and count bugs in the fluorescent lights.

...13-74-75-76...

Then she said, "Yes, you can address the entire school."

"Really?" I said.

"Really," she said. "But first, there are a few things you should know about Boogie."

And she told me. And now I'm about to tell the whole school.

Is my zipper up?

Public speaking freaks me out. I get nervous and sweaty. The butterflies in my stomach start kickboxing.

You wouldn't think butterflies could be that noisy.

But you'd be wrong.

"You're going to be okay," said Grimm, floating next to me.

"You don't know that," I whispered.

"Just tell them how sorry I am, without—you know—telling them I'm right beside you. Tell them our story. It's a good story."

He was right. It *was* a good story. It was about life and death. It had danger and intrigue. And a cat named Hurl. And best of all, it was about how Boogie was a good guy who deserved a chance.

That's what I told the assembly. I also told them about Grimm. About how we were best friends. I told them about the Totally To-Do List. How we never finished it. But how now I wanted to finish it. Then I told them about how one of the to-do's was to be a hero.

I spotted Boogie in the audience. He looked like he was trapped on a hostile planet and the transporter was down. He looked scared.

"The first step to being a hero is to not think of yourself as a hero. Because it's lame. No one goes around thinking what a hero he or she is."

LOOK AT ME, BEING A HERO!

LOOKIN' GOOD!

LOOKIN' SHARP!

LOOKIN' ALL HERO-Y *

HERO →

* A WORD I JUST MADE UP.

"No, the best way to be a hero is to just do the right thing. Even when it's hard. Especially when it's hard."

I continued, "Sometimes we're told some kids are one thing when they're really something different. Sometimes we all believe the lie. And spread the lie to other people. Even when we all know it's a lie. It's fun to make stuff up about someone. It's fun because it's not happening to us. It's happening to them. It's happening to Boogie."

All the kids in the auditorium turned and looked at Boogie. He started to sweat.

Grimm leaned in. "You're doing great."

"Heroes tell the truth. And the truth is that kids who we lie about are great kids. They can do stuff like draw really well. Their parents own a bowling alley, and they once lived in Canada. They speak French. And they might have the world's record for the largest bubble gum bubble."

The crowd went, "Whoa."

"I made that last part up. Which is easy, when no one knows anything about someone."

Grimm leaned in again. "Tell them it was me. It was all my fault. Tell them I'm sorry."

"My friend Grimm made up all that stuff about Boogie. Like the raised-by-bears thing and the eating-paper-clips thing. He thought he was being clever, but he was just being mean. I'm pretty sure, wherever he is, he knows that now."

"I do!" said Grimm. "Also, I'm right here. But don't tell them that."

"And he's sorry," I said. "Really, really sorry."

Grimm nodded. "I am. I really, really am."

I continued, "And I'm sorry too. I believed Grimm's lies when I should have known better. I teased Boogie too. I laughed at him. Just like all of you did. So, while I'm in detention for the rest of my life, I'd like all of you to reconsider someone you may have dismissed. Someone with a big heart. And a big smile."

"Boogie for student council president!" yelled a kid.

The kids chanted, "Boogie! Boogie! Boogie!"

Boogie sat there staring at me. He looked a bit angry, but also a bit surprised. As the kids continued chanting, he finally smiled. He had a nice smile. It was a bit shaky. But even though he was out of practice, his smile lit up his whole face.

I turned to Grimm. He was smiling too.

Well, this was it. If anything was going to get Grimm on his way, this was it. I turned to look at him. Any second now . . .

Any second . . .

He was still there.

Just when I was coming to terms with the idea that I was going to be haunted by my best friend for the rest of my life, there was a voice from the audience.

"Fix the water fountain on the second floor!" yelled a voice.

Then another voice yelled, "Taco Tuesdays on Mondays, Wednesdays, Thursdays, and Fridays!"

A cheer began to slowly build.

One more voice. "No more standardized tests!"

And the cheer swelled into a roar.

Well, I had done it. I'd made Boogie popular. Everyone liked him. Everyone loved him. Everyone wanted something from him.

I'd totally ruined his life.

CHAPTER 29

Sometimes you try to do the right thing for the right reasons. And sometimes you try to do the right thing for the wrong reasons. And sometimes you do the wrong thing for the right reasons. But this time I managed to do the wrong thing for the wrong reasons.

I made Boogie popular.

I made Boogie miserable.

I made Boogie run and hide.

But where?

"He ran backstage!" said Grimm.

I turned and looked. Boogie was fleeing through the stage door, but it was blocked by the janitor, Mr. Glenn.

Which is to say, it was *totally* blocked.

Boogie stopped, turned, and faced the audience.
He looked terrified.

Ms. Spitzcracker, Grimm, and I started to move toward Boogie. Boogie looked left, right, down, and finally up.

He was headed upward toward the catwalk above the stage. I climbed after him.

Meanwhile, Grimm was floating along right beside me.

"You've got to stop him," yelled Grimm. "Boogie could get hurt. He could slip and fall!"

I climbed faster.

As I climbed, I kept an eye on Boogie. He reached the catwalk and climbed on.

"Boogie, stop!" I yelled.

But he didn't stop. He slowly started inching his way down the narrow walkway. I looked past him. The catwalk came to a dead end.

There was nowhere for him to go.

I got to the top of the ladder and inched out onto the catwalk. Then I made a rookie mistake. I looked down.

There's a reason they tell you not to look down. Your stomach falls to your shoes. Which is a very bad look, and really not fair to your shoes.

"Boogie, stop!" I yelled.

Boogie looked back at me. "Stay away!"

I stopped. I took a deep breath. I looked straight at Boogie.

I continued, "I get it now. You don't need to be popular. It's not worth it. You're fine the way you are. Forget about student council president. I'll tell everyone not to vote for you. You can go back to being the old Boogie. I'll even tell everyone you really were raised by bears. Although they might not believe that now. We may have to change it to raccoons."

"Raccoons?" said Grimm.

"I'm doing the best I can!" I yelled.

"You're talking to Grimm again, aren't you?" said Boogie.

I said, "No! Yes. I don't know. Maybe."

"That's pretty weird," said Boogie.

"Yes," I agreed.

"Sometimes I wish I had someone to talk to," said Boogie.

"You can talk to me," I offered.

Boogie arched an eyebrow. "You just tried to ruin my life."

"I mean, you know, after I stop ruining your life, we could start talking."

Boogie smiled. "I'd like that."

I reached out my hand. "Me too."

Boogie grabbed my hand and started inching his way down the catwalk. I glanced at the audience. They looked like they were watching *Avengers: Middle School Wars* and they had just discovered that Thanos had been raised by raccoons.

Boogie had almost reached me when he slipped a little. I let go of the railing and reached out with my other hand to steady him. Big mistake.

Okay. Not good. For several reasons.

1. NEGATIVE UPPER BODY STRENGTH
2. LAST PLACE IN ROPE CLIMBING
3. LONG WAY TO FLOOR
4. ONE TOO MANY DEAD PEOPLE ALREADY

I looked up. Boogie was staring down at me. He was frozen in place. He clearly wanted to help me, but he couldn't. He was scared. I was scared. And . . . I was losing my grip.

I looked up again. Grimm was next to Boogie, and he was yelling.

But Boogie couldn't hear him.

Meanwhile, my hands were slipping. I tried to hang on, but I could feel my arms and legs cramping.

Just as I was about to let go, I looked up again.

251

Boogie could see Grimm! How was that possible? Then again, how was any of this possible? Maybe I should stop asking so many questions.

Boogie crawled over the railing and grabbed another rope. What happened next was cooler than any Avengers movie, because it was live and in REAL 3D!

It was over. Boogie let go, and we dropped a few inches to the stage. I was safe. Boogie was safe. And Grimm?

Still here.

"Are you okay?" asked Boogie.

"Yeah. You?" I said.

"Yeah."

"Well, that was epic."

"Too epic."

"I'm sorry about all this."

Boogie pointed up at Grimm. "I think I under-stand."

"Larry!" cried a girl's voice, in a way I never imag-ined a girl could cry my name.

It was Christi Mathison, and she was running right toward me.

Wow. Did that just happen?
I looked up. "Grimm, did you see that? Grimm?"
I looked all around.

GRIMM?... GRIMM?...

EPILOGUE

Grimm moved on.

Was it the kiss? Or helping Boogie? Or helping me?
I have no idea.

I miss him. Especially during detention. Grimm
could be annoying, but nothing is more annoying
than detention.

123... 124... 125...

Boogie went back to being Boogie. Except no one
gives him a hard time anymore. Oh, and he wasn't
elected student council president.

Christi and I hang out sometimes. No more kissing.

But some really interesting conversations.

I went back to see Dr. Hank a few times. We talked about Grimm and me. And everything I'd been through.

And then there's Hurl. We hang out a lot in the treehouse. Which is to say that I hang out, and Hurl throws up a lot.

It was pretty quiet in the treehouse without Grimm. I missed him. Both the alive Grimm and the ghost Grimm. Grimm could be annoying (both the living and life-like versions). But it was a fun kind of annoying. That insult-each-other, punch-each-other-in-the-shoulder, see-who-can-spit-farther kind of fun.

Sure, I'd lost a good friend. Twice. But I gained a new one.

Boogie's not exactly the same as Grimm. Not better. Or worse. Just different. We started spending a lot of time together. Sometimes at his family's bowling lanes.

Bowling is a lot harder than it looks.

Things are pretty much back to normal. I do spend a lot of time thinking about Grimm. Sometimes I even think I see him.

But I don't. It's just the wind. Or Mr. Sniggles. Or Hurl snoring.

Cats are weird.

Grimm is gone. And that's sad. But it's also okay. He was here, but he wasn't here. He was real, but not real. He was in the world. But not of the world.

He was a ghost.

And ghosts don't belong here. They belong someplace where they can be themselves. Fully themselves.

Grimm belongs in a place where he can achieve total Grimm-ness.

I like to think he's very happy.

And that makes me happy.

Photo courtesy of the author

MICHAEL FRY is the best-selling author of the James Patterson Presents How to Be a Supervillain series. A cartoonist for over thirty years, Michael is the cocreator and writer of the *Over the Hedge* comic strip, which was turned into a DreamWorks film starring Bruce Willis and William Shatner. He lives near Austin, Texas. Visit him online at overthehedgeblog.wordpress.com.